THE BUBBLE LADY

BY JANICE OATES

Illustrated by Debora Cordero Martinez

THE BUBBLE LADY

Copyright © 2020 by Janice Oates
ISBN 978-1-7345235-3-9

Designed and Published by King's Daughter Publishing
Indian Trail, North Carolina 28079
www.KingsDaughterPublishing.com

Illustrated by Debora Cordero Martinez

Printed in the United States of America.

DEDICATION

This book is dedicated with love
to my granddaughter Julia and grandson Justice!
~ Love, Gaga

ACKNOWLEDGEMENTS

Thank you to my Heavenly Father, God, my Savior and Lord, Jesus Christ, and the Holy Spirit who empowered me to write "The Bubble Lady."

Thank you to my co-workers who allowed me to provide a small act of kindness in blowing bubbles every Friday afternoon to help them get through their day.

This book would not have been possible without the loving support and encouragement of my husband, Jerry Oates, Sr. I love you.

For understanding the long hours and taking a break from our mother and son dates, I thank my children, Jerry Jr. and Jerrell. Momma loves you.

For motivation when I was feeling overwhelmed and for providing a listening ear, thank you to my daughter-in-love, Natasha. Mother-in-love loves you.

To Debora C. Martinez, you are truly a gifted artist. Thank you for sharing your gift of beautiful illustrations.

To S. Kristi Douglas of King's Daughter Publishing, words cannot express my gratitude to you for your love, prayers, words of encouragement and perseverance on this journey. You are a blessing indeed, a special jewel. You never left my side. Thank you for sharing your wisdom, expertise and numerous resources. Thank you for the beautiful front and back book cover design.

Thank you to Tynetta Hare, an answer to my prayers. When I didn't know the first place to look for a publisher, it was through you that I was introduced to S. Kristi Douglas. I'm forever grateful. I love you "Beautiful."

To my parents, siblings, other family members, mentors and friends, thank you for your endless prayers and love. Thank you for inspiring me to never give up on my dreams. Don't give up on yours.

I love you all.

One bright, sunny, summer morning, Susan, her mother and some friends loaded up her mother's red van with a picnic basket of food and a large, brightly colored blanket. The blanket was red and orange, hand-crocheted by Susan's grandmother, and was only used for special occasions.

On this special day, Susan and her friends were headed to a neighborhood park for a picnic. After enjoying lunch, they decided to take a walk around the park.

Across the lawn, Susan noticed something surprising. She saw a woman dressed in a bright red shirt with big blue bubble dots on it. She recognized the woman's attire. All the children loved it.

"Look! Here comes The Bubble Lady!" shouted Susan. The Bubble Lady had just finished celebrating a child's birthday party. She often helped with birthday celebrations.

"I've been waiting all year to see her!" said Susan. Susan asked her mother if she and her friends could go meet The Bubble Lady. Susan's mother agreed. The Bubble Lady loved to have fun and brought joy to everyone she met.

Susan and her friends ran toward The Bubble Lady and crowded around her. It was the first time her friends had ever seen or heard of her. "Shhhh! Quiet down!" whispered Susan. "Or she won't do the bubbles." "Okay," whispered Susan's friends.

The Bubble Lady heard Susan trying to calm her friends. "Hi Susan! It's so nice to see you again," said The Bubble Lady. "It's been a year since we've seen one another. How are you?" she asked.

"I'm great!" said Susan, smiling widely. "Who are these happy faces?" asked The Bubble Lady. "These are my friends," said Susan. "My mother brought us to the park for a picnic. We were just finishing our lunch and decided to take a walk around the park when we saw you," she said. Susan wondered if The Bubble Lady would blow bubbles for her and her friends too.

Before she could even ask, The Bubble Lady answered, "Of course! I'll blow bubbles for you and your friends. I love to bring joy, fun, happiness and excitement to all the boys and girls. I'm here to help lift your spirits and put smiles on your faces." The Bubble Lady laughed as she twirled around, raising her arms to the sky. Even her laughter sounded like bubbles! Bubbles began to swirl in the wind as she spun around.

The Bubble Lady sat on her blanket on the lawn and encouraged the children to join her. Even though they were excited, they sat right away. They didn't want to miss anything!

The Bubble Lady thought she should go over a few rules. The rules were to be obedient, cooperative, have respect for one another, and wait for permission to stand. "Do you think you'll be able to obey all the rules?" she asked. "Yes, Bubble Lady!" shouted the children. "Good! Now let's have some fun!" she said. The children began to jump up and down with joy. Some were even running in circles!

The Bubble Lady picked up a huge bottle of bubbles and opened it. She pulled out a bubble wand and began to blow short breaths into the wand as she held it high in the sky. Then she lowered the wand and waved it back and forth. Bubbles were everywhere! Out came the bubbles, both big and small. Up, up and away they went! There were so many shapes and sizes! Some popped right away. Others lingered for what seemed like forever!

The children's eyes stretched wide with amazement and they tried to reach up and touch the bubbles. The Bubble Lady was having so much fun blowing bubbles that she forgot to ask the children to stand and join her. "Oh my!" she said, joyfully. "This is so much fun! Up, up and away they go!" said The Bubble Lady.

She started to dip the wand back into the bubble solution to refill and blow again. She could see the children's excitement in their eyes. "Come children, come! Join in the fun with the bubbles!"

One of the children asked, "Will you give us some bubbles to take home?" The Bubble Lady said she would give everyone bubbles. She had plenty. After all, she was The Bubble Lady!

"Here's a container of bubbles for each of you," said The Bubble Lady. "Remember to use short breaths, now."

The bubble wands were multicolored. Some were blue and some were red. The children blew the bubbles quite easily. Some tried to reach out and catch them.

"Oops! Be careful not to trample one another!" said The Bubble Lady. "This is so much fun, isn't it?" Susan asked her friends. "It sure is!" they said.

Susan's friends thanked her for introducing them to The Bubble Lady. "You're welcome," said Susan. She thanked her friends for coming to the picnic in the park with her. She was glad her mother could bring them.

"This has been the best picnic in the park that I've ever been to," said one of Susan's friends. "Oh, I'm so glad," said Susan. "We had so much fun with The Bubble Lady!"

Finally, Susan's mother said it was time to go home. "Awwwwww," said Susan and her friends. They were having fun and were disappointed to leave.

"Thank you, Bubble Lady! You helped make this the best picnic in the park," said Susan's friends. "You're welcome. It was my pleasure!" said The Bubble Lady. "Thank you, Susan, for inviting me to your picnic. You have all been such great fun to blow bubbles with," she said.

"Goodbye, Bubble Lady," said Susan and her friends as they waved.

"Goodbye!" said The Bubble Lady. "See you next time!"

ABOUT THE AUTHOR

Janice Oates lives in Charlotte, North Carolina. She loves children and is a Sunday school teacher of 23 years. Delivered from feelings of rejection, her passion and love for Christ compels her to reach out to youth. As a mentor, Janice created the program "U R First" to provide self-esteem workshops to elementary students. Her desire is to use her God-given gifts and talents to impact the lives of youth and families. "The Bubble Lady" is her first children's book. To order more copies or to request an appearance by the author, visit: **www.JaniceOates.com** or Email: **Janice.Oates60@gmail.com**.

ABOUT THE ILLUSTRATOR

Illustrator **Debora Cordero Martinez** is a visual artist from Florida. From a young age, she displayed a love for art. The cartoons, music, environments, and cultures she grew up with continue to mold her current style and visions. Upon attending Duke University, Debora has expanded both her interests and skills in art. She recognized the lack of and need for proper representation of people of color in arts and media. Today she actively works to uplift these communities in her artistic endeavors.

CPSIA information can be obtained
at www.ICGtesting.com
Printed in the USA
BVHW021348010920
587772BV00015B/72